darling two hearts

s{e}an?

Published simultaneously in the United States and
Great Britain in 2017 by Pretend Genius
Copyright © Sean Brijbasi

ISBN: 978-0-9995277-1-9

other books by Sean Brijbasi

One Note Symphonies
for Emma

Still Life in Motion
for those who play
Marius and Andréus

The Unknowed Things
for Julius

The Dictionary of Coincidences, Volume i
for Emma

S{E}AN?
for EM{M}A+

E{M}MA+ the ghost orchids
for Emma

for e{m}ma+ the ghost orchids

matter

"I live to express myself freely in creation."

--Lee Jun-fan

1: Invention Gardens

i

I wait until everyone else gets on the train. I can't read my book while the train is moving because I get dizzy. I soak up as many of the words as I can so I'll have interesting thoughts while I'm going home or going to work or going to meet friends. So I wait until the very last second when the train doors are about to close. I never know what the words will do to me or what interesting thoughts I'll have and I don't want to miss a single word.

Reading my own book on the train makes me dizzy but I read over other people's shoulders while the train is moving with only a slight nausea that I overcome by turning away for a few seconds and shaking my head.

I think people dislike other people reading over their shoulder but I can't help myself. If I see someone reading a book on the train I'll try to move behind them at the precise angle necessary to get a clear view of what they're reading. It's become second nature to me and I think that I'm the best in the world at it. I know there are challengers out there and I imagine train riders in Barcelona or Lagos or Santiago peering over the shoulders of unwitting readers.

Sometimes it's not possible to read someone else's book and I just stand or sit and think whatever interesting thoughts my own book has left me with. I also sometimes think interesting thoughts that I have left myself with.

Sometimes the book the other person is reading is not interesting to me. I can't begin to explain my disappointment. I don't think less of the person because he or she is reading a book I don't like. Who knows why people read what they read at any given moment in their life? I'm just disappointed because it's not something I would read at that moment in my life. Sometimes I feel very sad for the person reading the book. This happens more often than you might think.

I had often thought about writing a novel about reading over other people's shoulders. In the novel the books that the main character reads would start to describe his own life. The text would be ambiguous enough to possibly not be about his own life but there would be enough details added to make the text convincing. Eventually the text in the various books he would read over other people's shoulders would start to describe his future. There would be several futures. Confusion ensues until a conclusion is reached. I think a woman and several children are involved.

ii

There are a few others like me on the trains. You probably don't notice us. We sometimes glance at each other before returning to the other person's book we are reading. We don't do it to acknowledge each other—as if we are giving each other a secret signal—but only out of curiosity about the book the other person is reading. Is it philosophy? Literature? Poetry? What words being put together for the first time have I not read that they are reading?

Alas, when we are reading over someone's shoulder we can only read what is in front of the person in front of us. I can say that I have never been caught reading over someone's shoulder but I have seen a few others who have been caught. So I have never felt the shame (if it is shame) involved in this so-called transgression though I know in my heart that one day it will happen.

iii

I stop at Invention Gardens to go to the grocery store. My favorite grocery store (I think we each have one) is two blocks away from the Invention Gardens Train Stop. It's called Invention Gardens Food Shop. I like being at the grocery store. When one visits a grocery store for the first time the landscape is unknown. We don't know where the vegetables are. We can't find the bread. But after our third or fourth visit the location of where the vegetables and the bread are is in our head and we know the paths we have to take to successfully find all the items on our list in the shortest amount of time possible.   There are more esoteric items (caviar, for example) that we never map but we don't buy caviar often (if ever).   But it is important to remember that caviar is also a food item just like any other food item in the grocery store (like a book we haven't read that we keep on our bookshelf at home). I sometimes forget an item on my list and I have to go back four or five aisles to find it. I do this without frustration. I want people to feel that a grocery story is something more than a necessity although I don't take any action in this regard.

I used to come to this grocery store when I was a child. It wasn't far from my elementary school. But you would be mistaken to think (if you think) that I have not travelled far because I live so near to the elementary school I attended as a child.

The grocery store had a different name then and was smaller. Whenever my mother or father gave me some change I would stop in on my way home and buy candy from the candy machine.   I sometimes saw teenagers stealing from the ice cream freezer located at the front of the store. One boy would stand in front of the freezer door while another boy reached behind him, pulled the door open, and took out whatever ice cream bars he could get his hands on. The boys gave the ice cream to the girls who waited outside the grocery store. I liked the girls because they spoke a few words to me from time to time. I felt safe when I saw them (even though the boys they were with scared me).

iv

The trip from the train stop closest to my apartment—the Avenue of Children—to Invention Gardens doesn't provide a lot of time and opportunity for reading. It's a short trip (only two stops) and there usually aren't many people on the train as it leaves the Avenue of Children.

But a few weeks ago I did see a woman (I might describe her later) reading a book. I noticed the book immediately. It's difficult to maneuver next to someone or behind someone when there aren't many people on the train. I often carry a map of the city with me and get close to someone to ask for directions. This pretense is an ordeal and rarely works because I feel like I must move away after my subterfuge and my chance is missed unless there is a large population of people who get on the train at the following stop. As I move away I feel as if I'm falling into the darkness of a deep well from where I can see the light above getting dimmer and dimmer as I descend. I think I end up feeling worse than if I had never tried. And yet I can't help but feel that there might be a chance. I think this is the normal type of desperation that all people feel when they want something very badly.

I had planned on getting off the train at Invention Gardens to go to the grocery store but when I saw that the woman (and her book) stayed on the train I stayed on the train also. I stayed on the train for as long as she stayed on the train. And when she finally departed at the Hanami Park station it had been three glorious stops in between.

from The Love of Woman and The Love of Man

The renaissance was a time when art and science grew. All over Europe scientific discoveries were being made. The most important invention during the renaissance was the printing press which made it easier for people to find out about new discoveries and inventions. The scientific method was created and the human body became better understood. Wil)l#iam Sh!ak3espear/e lived during this time. He wrote dozens of plays and poems. His plays were based on everyday life and true historical facts and showed that humans were the cause of many comedies and tragedies.

v

You have to understand that when I am reading over someone's shoulder I must read at their pace. I can't turn the page for them or tell them to wait until I am finished reading the last paragraph. I must quickly become attuned to their reading gait.

I was, for my first few months of reading over other people's shoulder, choppy in my attunement. I was sometimes too slow, sometimes too fast. But after many weeks of reading over other people's shoulders I became attuned. I understood based on their breathing how fast their eyes moved across the page. I knew what a scratch of the head or a caress of the chin meant. I deciphered every fidget, every shift. You could say that for several stops on a train ride I had become as much one with another human being who was a stranger to me as anyone could be. I sometimes read faster because I didn't want to miss a single word but that was never my intention. I wanted to read at the same pace. I wanted to finish the last word on a page just before the page was turned.

I didn't always know what was happening in a book that I was reading over someone's shoulder because I could only read the few pages or paragraphs that were available to me during the train ride. I didn't know the plot or the major theme. I didn't know if the dialogue contained within those few pages was between protagonist and antagonist or the mumblings of other minor characters. But it didn't matter. I couldn't help myself.

from Blood K

I didn't call out to her but I did have (what one might call) a revelation. Suppose the strange marking was always there beneath my skin—since I was born—and for some reason seeped through my body's dermatological layers over time until it was visible to me? I thought about what I would say to a doctor. I wasn't sure but I hoped that any doctor would shrug and say they saw those kinds of strange markings all the time, that they weren't so strange, and that they would go away eventually. The markings looked strange but they were just random spots. A skin affliction perhaps.

2: Hanami Park

i

The train wasn't crowded so I took out my map of The 6 Cities and asked the woman where the Flower Viewing Statue was located. She surprised me and told me that she was also new to the city and that she too was going to see the Flower Viewing statue. She put her book into her bag.

"What are you reading?" I asked her.

"Dreams of terrible angels", she said. "It's quite good."

I had already read the book and she was, in my opinion, correct. The book was quite good and probably still was after a second reading. But I wasn't interested in reading it again just yet. Don't get me wrong. When I am reading over someone's shoulder it happens sometimes that the person is reading a book I have already read. I don't always notice right away. And who knows? Sometimes I may not notice at all because I don't always have the opportunity to see the title of the book. The words we read alone in our room seem different on a train or in a park or in another building. Even our eyes are different in different places. But since I already knew what she was reading I had lost my interest in reading over her shoulder to read it again.

"There it is", she pointed on the map. "At the Hanami Park stop."

"I see", I said. "Thank you. I didn't mean to bother you."

"It's okay", she said.

She took out her book and started reading again. I know I said I wasn't interested in reading *Dreams of Terrible Angels* over someone's shoulder again but I couldn't resist. It was a hardback book and the print was larger than usual and inviting. You could even say it looked juicy. But I could only read over her shoulder for a few paragraphs.

The train continued on and made its stops during which time more people entered and the space between the woman and me increased as the carriage became filled up. I could still see her between the heads and over the shoulders of the other passengers. When the train reached the

Hanami Park stop I watched her get off. I stayed on the train for one more stop (more on this later). I would take the longer walk to Hanami Park from there. I wanted to meet her again but I wanted to meet her walking from another direction.

ii

I got off the train at the stop after the Hanami Park stop. I had three blocks to walk to reach Hanami Park and the Flower Viewing statue. I imagined the woman walking leisurely around the park taking in all the flowers and plants before making her way to the statue itself. That is how I believe most people navigated Hanami Park because that is how I navigated Hanami Park when I first visited. I calculated that she would be at the park for a minimum of thirty minutes which gave me time to walk to the Flower Viewing statue.

As for why I stayed on the train for the extra stop? It is as I said that I wanted to meet the woman from another direction but I was also lucky in that a man who had gotten on the train was reading a book at the perfect angle for me to read over his shoulder. He was reading a book of poetry and the short poems that he read, as the train stopped and started, added more meaning to my day.

iii

I ran up the stairs from the train station and out onto the street. I felt invigorated after reading over the man's shoulder. Reading poetry over someone's shoulder is different from reading a work of fiction because there is a context that is unavailable from reading the latter, therefore the invigoration. But the invigoration ends quickly, whereas the mystery of unanswered questions (caused by the lack of context) elicited from reading a work of fiction over someone's shoulder remains longer.

I also had a secret plan. I sometimes saw others who I thought had secret plans. All of my secret plans involved following people who read books.

It wasn't a consistently sunny day—mostly cloudy—although every now and then slivers of sunlight shone brightly through the thick-ish clouds. I tried to guess exactly where the light hit. Perhaps on Invention Gardens. When I am executing a secret plan I prefer rain to sun. I feel that I can show myself in the rain because I am more hidden.

I checked the traffic before I crossed the road and saw a man sitting on a bench reading a book in the small park on the other side. As I crossed over the man stood and walked to a bus stop. He kept reading. I felt excited. The bus he was catching would be going away from Hanami Park. I thought if I didn't go to Hanami Park immediately then the woman I met on the train would be gone and I might never see her again. But she was a slow reader. She would be reading *Dreams of Terrible Angels* for the next week if she read at the pace she was reading (taking into account the other routines of everyday life). If I didn't see her on the train for a few days then maybe she would have finished the book in that time and started on another book that I hadn't read.

When I say that the woman was a slow reader I don't mean it as a criticism. She read at the same pace that I also wanted to read. I felt, as I was reading over her shoulder for that brief amount of time, that she read with love. If she and I lived an ocean apart and started reading the same book at the very same moment and continued reading without stopping we would finish reading on the exact same word at the exact same time (even saying the last word aloud as we closed the book).

from The City on the Edge of Town

It's twenty three after twelve and Joseph takes the escalators down to track fifteen to board a train heading north. Earlier, after he said good-bye to his children and before he bought his ticket, a man asked him: "Have you heard?"

Joseph was unable to answer. He was too tired to have heard. He was tired of listening, tired of talking, tired of having to know where he was, tired of accidentally overhearing people, and all of the other tireds he was too tired to think about. So he looked at the man without answering and walked to the bathroom. Inside he saw two men painting the wall adjacent to the sinks.

iv

I followed the man onto the bus. He sat down on a seat by the aisle. I couldn't have asked for him to take a better position. I stood behind him so that when he opened his book all the letters and words jumped out at me. I thought I would just read over his shoulder for one stop and if I ran from the next stop to Hanami Park I might still see the woman I met on the train. But he flipped through the pages of his book to a hand-written letter hidden between the last page and the back cover.

I thought a letter was strange because no one writes letters anymore. I won't tell you the contents of the letter but I think it made me feel sad. Without thinking I put my hand on the man's shoulder. He lurched sideways and looked up at me. The paper fell out of the book. I picked it up and handed it to him.

17

"Sorry", I said.

He put the piece of paper between the last page and the back cover and closed the book. The title of the book was *Observations on a Future Death* (a book I hadn't read). The bus stopped and I got off. I watched the bus move down the road like I might watch the earth from one of its naturally orbiting satellites while trying to imagine and understand the microscopic size of one human person living on it.

v

Every once in a while I will buy a book that I have started to read over someone's shoulder. It doesn't happen very often but I will tell you that my favorite parts of the books are always the parts that I have read over someone's shoulder. And I always remember which part I have read and without thinking I succumb to the same pace that I read that particular part of the book when I read that particular part of the book over someone's shoulder. In fact, the memory of the space around me and all that I see in my periphery come back to me whole.

I hurried along the street to Hanami Park. I don't like running in public so I walked a little faster than I usually did thinking that I would cut my walking time by at least a fourth. I looked to see if any buses were coming so that I would hop on a bus and reach Hanami Park faster. But I was caught in between stops. I increased my speed. Along the way I saw a family eating lunch on a restaurant patio. There was a man, a woman, a boy, and a girl. The girl's head was down and her long hair covered her face and everything below her face. But I knew from her lean in the chair and the angle of her head pointing downward that she was reading. I had very little time and it would have been a preposterous and bold attempt indeed to try to read over the girl's shoulder, especially with such long hair and her parents (most likely) sitting right across from her. I crossed the street to walk by them—to be close to her reading. The girl looked up as a truck drove by and for the briefest of moments I spied the book. I couldn't see the book title or read a word of it but I saw the page. I

walked by the family but turned around to take
another look at them.

I don't want you to think that I always shied
away from making preposterous and bold attempts.
I believed that such attempts honed my ability to
make more commonplace attempts.

I reached Hanami Park and searched for the
woman but I couldn't find her. There would be no
more reading over other people's shoulders on that
partly cloudy day. No more trains or buses or
walking. I wanted to sleep. Sometimes I like to
think that my ilk command the streets and scrap to
the end of time but even we grow weary. People
grow weary for different reasons.

from The Collected Verse of Moika Pikkakoika

You undress and the room is no longer naked.
The mirror on the dresser reveals
the freckles on the small of your back.

A thousand infinity is more than a hundred infinity.
A plane flies overhead and the plaster on the ceiling
unpeels above our cold bed.

No one can hear us. Our eyes stretch
to the universe along invisible filaments
that lift our heads up so that we might see
the stars.

3: Blackstar Station

i

I thought about the poems the man on the bus was reading. One of them stayed in my head for a few days. I'm sure I wasn't remembering it correctly but the way I was remembering it made me feel disconnected from the people around me. I felt as if my brain or a part of my brain somewhere between my eyes and an inch or two back was separate from the world in which I lived. Maybe it was the part that controlled my hands because I couldn't feel them the way I normally did.

The poem gave my day meaning. I said that. But why didn't my day have meaning before? And would it have had meaning without the poem? Maybe I was already too disconnected from the world and from the people around me to give meaning to my days without finding it in books.

But the poem stayed in my memory and connected to my present. Some memories don't connect to my present. They live in my brain as if they are in a medium-sized pot covered with a tight lid—never to get out, never to mingle with my current and future days. Each memory has its own pot, each memory an orphan trapped in its own orphanage. Orphan memories are good memories but more closely resemble nightmares when I try to picture the images of them in my brain. But I treat them like prisoners so what should I expect?

I started to forget about the poem. It started to degrade in my memory. The more I thought about the words in the poem the less meaning they had until I could feel my hands again.

from The Girl in the Corner

At the top of the hill beneath the fence there is a hand buried in the ground. Severed just above the wrist, you'll find it in a clear plastic bag. There will be dirt beneath the fingernails because it was useful in burying itself. If you hear dogs but can't see them, presume they are the hunting party organized by the local barber. His name is Picador Ralston and he's handy with a pair of scissors and a razor.

His favorite type of hair to cut is German with a seamless blend of recessive Flemish and South Eritrean underlocks. It's the way the scissors finishes the cut he says. He'll shave a beard if he has to but it's not his favorite thing to do.

The dogs will be a mix of setter and terrier. And—this is important—there will be a greyhound. Should they find you be unafraid. It will only be painful. If there is a woman in the hunting party, be sure to tell me. When you tell me about her don't be witty. There are differences when it comes to wit. Be matter-of-fact and plain spoken. You're one of those people whose wit I can only tolerate if we are in a group of people. It spares me the tedium of responding. I am being kind by calling it wit. Kindness is my one failing.

There have been rumours—I won't deny them— that the hand buried there belongs to an unlucky acquaintance of mine. This is untrue. I'll also add that the hand is not mine.

The top of the hill may remind you of a biblical scripture your Sunday school teacher read to you once from the testaments. This memory will give you the false impression that the sun is shining through the clouds and that all will be well. I'll also add that when you hear the dogs it means they've picked up your scent and are probably less than half a mile away.

But the hand has a phone number written on its palm. I'm almost ashamed to admit it but I can't remember the number and that's why, well, yes, it's shameful I know, but that's why I need you to find the hand. The hand is still fresh and the number should still be legible. Bring me the hand or bring me the number on the hand. And just in case you were wondering, Picador Ralston is not my barber.

ii

I sit at a small table by the window in my apartment. Hummingbirds feed from the hummingbird feeder I keep on the window sill. Sometimes only one. Sometimes two or three. From there I see people waiting at the bus stop located directly in front of the apartment building I

26

live in. I don't take this bus often because it goes in the opposite direction of the places I go.

Weeks had passed since I saw the woman I met on the train. Yes, I was still thinking about her. It happens that I become fixated on something irrelevant to my daily routine because this fixation is an interruption of my routine and makes me feel free. My daily routine is recognizable to most people because they have the same daily routine. I wake up, I go to work, I come home (repeat, etc). But as many of you know this is only part of the story. There can be peculiar happenings during and in between the activities of my daily routine, though very random and very rare. Most of the happenings during and in between the activities of my daily routine are also routine: I meet friends (I have friends), I read books, I go to concerts, I go to restaurants. Even those who have everything available to them cannot escape their routine. It could be worse. That's what happens outside. What happens inside is different. What happens inside (every person who has ever lived) can only be described as violence and chaos.

One morning I was sitting by the window looking out to the bus stop when I saw the woman I met on the train. She sat down on the bench. She was taking the bus in the opposite direction of the places I go—to the ruined part of the city where the empty parking lots and uninhabited buildings make the streets look like a museum of blundered architecture.

A strange feeling comes over me when I pass by the broken-down buildings and abandoned cars in that part of the city (the feeling is no longer strange but it was strange). There is a feeling of nostalgia stirred up by the city ruins where all that is run-down makes me think of home and all the rough and battered concrete (from a distance) seems soft and warm.

I got lost once thinking about a book I read over someone's shoulder and found myself in one of those buildings. I was tired from walking and wanted to rest. I sat on a broken chair that I propped up with a brick. I looked out onto the street through an opening that was once blocked by a wall upon which perhaps pamphlets and documents were pinned—documents about nutrition or money. I could look out into The 6 Cities and see all the way to the river that divided it.

iii

I have never told the story of the origin of my peculiar fixation but as with most fixations it started early and within the family unit. My mother would take us (my siblings and I) to school with her when she was at university. On the bus she would read whatever book for whatever class she was attending that morning or afternoon. I was a fidgety child and always required some form of stimulation whether it was a book, a conversation, a song, or a game. I couldn't read my own book on the bus because I became dizzy so I had to satisfy myself with looking out the window until one day my mother opened her text book about organic chemistry. I saw the pictures of, what I found out over the course of the year, were organic compounds and carbon atoms.

```
            H
            |
      H     C     H
       \   ‖   /
        C     C
        ‖     ‖
        C     C
       /   ‖   \
      H     C     H
            |
            H
```

And while I was fascinated by the hieroglyphic nature of the symbols, as if they were the language of another universe, my attention was drawn to the symbols I did understand for I had no understanding of this universe or any other universe regardless of my ignorance to the fact that those strange hieroglyphic symbols were being used to try to explain a small part of the very universe in which I lived and more deeply than the symbols I did understand. I sat next to her and read one word and then another and then another and realized that I could read the book my mother was reading with little, if any, nauseating side-effects. But I didn't have to read over my mother's shoulder. I sat right next to her and leaned into her arm. Over the next few weeks I attuned myself to her reading pace. I visit my mother several times a month and sometimes I sit next to her and pretend that I am watching a show while she is reading. Her reading pace is still the same.

I have already asked myself if as an adult, by reading over other people's shoulders, I am trying to recapture the feeling of leaning into my mother's arm and resting my head on her shoulder. I don't think so but I don't always know what I'm feeling.

iv

I have a job. It's part of my daily routine. I work as a mannequin at a clothes store near Night stop. I work four hours a day almost every day. I share this job with two other people. I saw an advertisement for it in the newspaper. I was one of many people who showed up and the manager asked us to put on a hat or a jacket from the store and to stand perfectly still for thirty minutes. I held a canteen to my mouth to make it look like I was drinking from it. I stood the most still. I only moved my eyes when I thought the manager wasn't looking. I like the idea of a mannequin because mannequins don't comment on anything. I don't

31

like being asked questions even if I know the answer. I don't like being in conversations where I am expected to speak. My job as a mannequin doesn't require speaking or commenting. Commenting is a special kind of speaking that I dislike the most because it makes what is being commented on less likable even when the comments provide insight into what is being commented on. As a mannequin I can be around people and not have to speak. Sometimes I am in the store window. Sometimes I am in the store on top of a podium against the wall.

from The Boy vs. The Ocean

I have miles to go in this skin but I'm at my best when there's nothing to do. Yesterday I couldn't understand why people notice certain things but today I can't understand why they don't. I only have this. A simple statement about how good it is to be happy. To be happy without giving any thought that one day it might end. Life is better when there's nothing to hope for. We'll create games for it and give them importance but losing only means starting over.

So we play and we run and we jump as high as we can only to land again. That's when the ground propelled us into the air and the earth turned faster to speed up our legs. I'm thinking about you now.

I'm thinking about you and the park bench before the sprawl where we looked at small buildings and heard the ocean behind them. The ocean coming to wipe the slate clean then stop in front of us before receding to leave us with miles of empty space.

But I think that one day the ocean will stop in front of us and not recede right away. We'll take a walk along its length to catch a glimpse of past days floating around like so much debris in there. We'll run our hands along the wall of water and you'll ask me if we will meet again. And I'll say that you and I shall always meet again. It's as ordinary as the sunrise. And we'll rise above the horizon, hand in hand, and walk towards this place and sit on this bench and each day watch the ocean get closer and closer until the day it finally carries us away.

V

The bus to the part of the city I don't visit often comes every half-hour on the hour. In that half-hour I changed my shirt three times and combed my hair. I took my camera and walked down the stairs (sometimes running) out into the street and across the road to the bus stop. I stood there pretending that I didn't recognize the woman, waiting for her to say something about our previous meeting. It started to rain but stopped. She said nothing. Maybe she was pretending too. I turned to her and asked her if she knew what time it was.

"It's two fifty-three", she said.

"Thanks", I said. "Another few minutes then. Did you finish reading the book?" I asked her.

She looked at me.

"I met you on the train a few weeks ago. You were going to the flower viewing statue", I said.

"Of course", she said. "I'm sorry. I've met so many people since I moved here."

"No worries", I said. "It looks like we're headed in the same direction. Where are you going?"

"I don't know", she said. "I've heard there's a place at the Blackstar Station stop where you can see the entire city so I'm going to try to find it and take some pictures. And yes, I did finish the book. I liked it."

I didn't know that anyone else knew about the place at Blackstar Station but I shouldn't be surprised. I'm not the only one who ventures out into the world alone, although it seems that we who venture out into the world alone rarely meet each other. The bus arrived.

"I know the stop we have to go to", I said.

"Great", she said. "Let's make a day of it then."

I sat next to her. Let's make a day of it. The words of an adventure. Anything could happen. I opened the bus window and a breeze blew in that travelled from me to her and then, I presume, throughout the rest of the bus so that everyone could share the feeling I was feeling. I thought

35

about two questions to ask her and I wasn't sure which one I should ask first.

1. What book are you reading?
2. How did you like the Flower Viewing statue?

The first question was a direct strike to her soul. The second question was one I already knew the answer to because as far as I knew everyone felt the same way about the Flower Viewing statue and if you weren't a sculptor then I'm not sure what you could say about it. It's possible that the sight of the Flower Viewing statue saved someone's life at some point. Such a person would have a deep story to tell but it didn't appear she was someone whose life needed saving. It was difficult to know for sure though and if her life did need saving it was probably good to know. So I asked question two.

"How did you like the flower viewing statue?" I asked.

As she was answering I was thinking about the books I would recommend to her.

"I loved it", she said. "I don't know how she did it."

Maybe *The World That Destroyed the World* or the one that came out just recently called *Theophilus God.* I hadn't read either of those two.

"I was actually trying to get your attention on the train after we talked but you didn't see me", she said.

I felt a deep sadness come over me.

vi

When one is overcome by a deep sadness it's as if one is lying on a bed in a dark room and when the monsters come, as they always do, they take pity on you. You even tell them to come back later when you are fit for scaring. I remembered that I was reading some poems over a man's shoulder on the train. The woman and I became separated by the crowd. But my day was given meaning by those poems. A meaningful day is surely worth something. But could my day have been given even more meaning if I saw her at the Flower Viewing Statue and she and I strolled together? How much meaning was enough? Maybe I would have talked about the poems I read which would have led to a conversation that elicited mutual revelations that entangled us in a way that would have been difficult to disentangle without at least a few more encounters (or possibly never). I didn't know. Or maybe the meaning would have dissipated altogether. Maybe I would have thought of something shallow while I was talking to her or, even worse, unsavory. Also, I didn't know how much meaning I could handle in one day. Maybe it would have been too much. Maybe my body was incapable of incorporating too much meaning. I had a meaningful childhood. Maybe that's all the meaning my body could hold.

"Is it okay if we go beyond our stop one stop and then walk from there?" I asked. "I see things that I might not have otherwise seen."

"I like that", she said.

We departed the bus at the stop after Blackstar Station. I felt there would be no disentanglement since we were not, as yet, entangled.

I had made a possibly catastrophic mistake by going beyond Blackstar Station. As we walked towards our destination I tried to find something worth seeing. It was my idea, after all, to go beyond our original stop because "I see things that I might not have otherwise seen" which possibly implied that she would also see things she might not have otherwise seen. But I didn't see anything I might not have otherwise seen while we were walking. I thought maybe my way of seeing had become distorted by the situation I found myself in.

"Why were you trying to get my attention on the train?" I asked.

"I was going to ask you if you wanted to go to the flower viewing statue together."

The deepest sadness ever overcame me and I started to notice things in rapid succession while we were walking.

"There's a mannequin lying on the sidewalk over there," I said.

"I saw that," she said.

She saw it too.

"There's a shirt hanging from the window over there," I said.

And we went on noticing different things as we walked. Sometimes we noticed the same things and sometimes we didn't. But the silence of noticing things by myself that made those moments more sacred was missing. My observations had instead become a list. I was noticing things for the sake of distraction.

We eventually reached our destination. Something had changed in the short time that we were walking. We had become entangled but our entanglement was followed by a sudden disentanglement and I wanted to be on the train reading over someone's shoulder—something I had never read before—something so stunning, so exhilarating that I would forget about noticing things for a long time.

We continued to walk and she touched me on my shoulder to direct my attention to a box of umbrellas she noticed. We walked over to them. We pulled them out one by one and put them back in one by one. They were all broken. It was then that I felt that we had yet to become entangled so the entanglement/disentanglement that I believed happened between us earlier never really happened. We left the umbrellas and continued walking. We finally reached our destination. We climbed the stairs until we reached the floor from where we could see The 6 Cities to the river that divided it.

viii

I think back to all the times that I have read over someone's shoulder. I ask myself if I am doing something wrong. Am I hurting the people who are reading their books? Am I taking something from them that they don't want to give to me or to anyone else? Perhaps they don't want to share the moments of their reading. But I had often felt jealous of those who read on the train. Not just because they read on the train without feeling sick. I sometimes imagined reading a book on the train and someone else reading over my shoulder and then, at the end of some passage we have just read

41

together, we look at each other in silence because we have read words and sentences so stunning, so revelatory that there is no other way to express what we are feeling but to look at another human being in silence. And then I leave the train and the other person leaves the train and maybe we never see each other again or, if we do, we see each other only in passing as he or she is walking down the stairs to the canal or browsing for hats and scarves at the hat and scarf shop and neither of us can be sure that we remember the other.

The woman and I stood near the edge of the opening in the building and looked out to the city—the city that was hers and that was also mine. The moment reminded me of a page in a book that I read over someone's shoulder. I didn't remember (if I ever knew) the name of the book but the page I read described the scene of a man and a woman who had survived a bombing of their city and found each other. They found a pair of scissors in the debris and spent the night out in the open air cutting each other's hair. I remembered hearing, in the silence of my head, the sound of each snip of the scissors. I don't know what happened on the next page.

The woman took out her camera and took photographs of the city. She turned to me and took my photograph. She asked me to stand in front of the opening so she could take a photograph of me again (two photographs) with the city behind me. I asked her if she wanted me to take a photograph of her. I took three. Looking through the camera at her reminded me of a scene from another book (*Gorman y Vasquez*) I read over someone's shoulder on a long train ride to World A. It described a man who worked as a cashier at a diner. He looked through a plastic straw at a woman who had just walked through the door. In his mind he called her his *strawbaby*—alone in there and unaware of her special place in the world. She wore blue-jean shorts and a rose-colored top. Her eyes were brown and her hair was brown. And she was as beautiful as the most beautiful word in all the human languages for beauty.

I had forgotten about these particular books I had read over other people's shoulders. I panicked.

I wondered if I should catalogue them now that they were coming back to me. I never walked around with anything to write with. I just had to remember them. Could I? Would it be possible to remember later today after we returned home what I had remembered there?

I started to wonder if I was taking something away from the readers whose books I secretly occupied. I reasoned with myself that if I didn't remember and document what I had read over other people's shoulders then perhaps I was taking something away from them and making it meaningless.

It was time to return home. As we entered the bus the woman stepped on the back of my shoe and I felt the sole come loose. I didn't think she noticed because she didn't say anything. I sat down. Her name was Maria. When we reached our stop I told her I had to go to the grocery store and that I would be continuing on with my journey. And then I told her, as she stood up to leave, that I lived in the apartment building across the street from the bus stop where we met and that if I was at home and she wanted me to go on the bus with her again that she only had to call up to me. I would leave the window open anytime I was available. I think she said "okay" but the sound of the bus door opening and the traffic noise made it difficult to hear.

from Dreams of Terrible Angels

Mademoiselle reeled from the accusation. She couldn't believe that she, of all people, could be packaged in such a terse and provincial box that included the words horse, arm, pestilence, and gelatinous. It was only the other day she received a letter from an old school friend, full of expression about how bon-bon it was that she had unboxed herself three years prior on a hunting trip with the former Duke of Chalmers. So the gall, the nerve, the bottle-nosed dolphin nuts it took for him to rebox her made her feel a sickness she hadn't felt in some time. The turtlebum could have accused anyone, but why her? The gall again.

"Why?" she asked. "Why?"

And he, silent as a pecan, shrugged his skinny shoulders and faced his palms toward her to drain her of her powers.

"Je:su^s Ch4rist, you make me feel sick", she finally said. "Just."

He feigned remorse by looking down but he was a trickster who liked dulling the twinkle of the innocent and the unaware. She was the latter, for though it wasn't obvious to the unbridled chum, she had suddenly felt unboxed again and her sense of revulsion at the accusation softened. It wasn't long before she felt enough satisfaction to go on her way. But without realizing it, she had been drained of her powers and succumbed to his unfailing manipulations.

4: World A

i

I woke up on Sunday morning to the sound of rain. I opened the window and felt the air on my skin. I looked askance at the bus stop across the street. I didn't see any human figures standing there. Many Sundays and other days had gone by in such a way. It was a long time before I saw Maria again. I thought back to what I had done that might have kept her away. The 6 Cities seemed so small but it was big enough to never see someone again. Maybe she had gone away on an early holiday. It was the end of spring and the start of summer. The quality of books I read over people's shoulders always diminished during the summer. I think because there is this particular type of reading called 'summer reading' that is light and shallow. Sometimes summer reading is necessary even during other seasons.

During those many weeks that I didn't see her I tried to become someone else. For years an older woman who lived across the hall from me called me by a name other than the one given to me by my parents. I never corrected her. I liked the way she said the name. I could tell she liked saying the name. She never missed an opportunity to call behind me if I was walking down the hall or if she saw me anywhere on the street. Then one day she was gone. And I wondered if while in the process of disappearing that among all the images she could remember and all the sounds she could remember and all the people's faces she could remember and all the names she could remember that she remembered my face and thought of that name which wasn't mine.

After she disappeared I tried to become the name that she called me. I wasn't sure how to go about becoming another name but maybe people will think differently of me as that name. I thought of anyone I knew who went by the name (real or unreal) and searched for any similarities they had. I thought about the way the woman treated me so I could build the name's personality. It seemed to be a self-assured name and she treated me as if I knew what I was doing. She often asked for advice about some small matter that I usually shrugged off because I didn't have any answers for her. I think she only ever called to me from behind as I was walking away from her. I also used that as a clue for how I should act as the new name. I thought that's how I would behave with that particular name—I knew the answers but didn't have time to share them with others because I was industrious.

It was difficult to read over other people's shoulders as the new name. I had become impatient. One time when I was trying to become the name I reached out my hand and turned the page for someone. He looked at me. I looked him straight in his eyes and said "faster". He closed the book and moved away from me. The other person's reading gait no longer mattered to me. I can say that being the other name was disruptive to my soul.

I didn't go to work on the day I turned the page. I had crossed the line as the new name and who knows what I would have done at work. I didn't think the name would allow me to stand completely still. I went back home. I became myself with my real name again. When I reached my apartment I knocked on the door across the hall to see if the lady had returned but there was no answer. I wanted to tell her my real name so she would stop calling me by a name that wasn't mine.

from Mumb

I compare two lives with the patterns observed by Triameches. Penta was the goddess of rooms. When she was alive (all gods die) many rooms were built in her honor. Rooms were built even during times of war and especially during times of war because destroyed rooms had to be replaced (Penta the insatiable). The first room built in Penta's honor was by Darda the Mumbler who wanted a quiet place to be left alone so he could mumble without being disturbed. Triameches observed the patterns of all the rooms ever built in honor of Penta (Triameches the observer).

One day at work when I was standing completely still (overlooking the long rack of short-sleeved shirts) I heard the bell that rang when a new customer entered the store through the front door. I usually didn't look up immediately when I heard the bell. I gave the customer a chance to look around the store to make sure their attention was turned away from me before I looked to see who it was.

The only activities I could do at work besides standing completely still were watching and thinking. And more and more I was thinking—or should I say I was feeling (so I also did some feeling) that my life was coming to an end and that it was okay. It might seem like the feeling didn't happen suddenly—that it happened over time while I was thinking at work but it did happen suddenly. One day without warning I suddenly felt that I had nothing to miss in this life, that I had given everything of myself to everyone, that I had loved everyone as much as I could ever love them, that I had lived as fully as I could have lived even if I would live for another hundred years. I didn't know with any certainty but that's how I felt. But I also felt that I would live for another hundred years and that the future (my future) had already been created inside of me.

I saw Maria out of my peripheral vision. She raised her arms to put her hair into a bun and it was the first time in my life that I stumbled (ever so slightly) while I was standing completely still. I became aware of my breathing. I felt that I missed some breaths and had to start over several times to restore my breathing to normal.

The days had become an unfilled outline of life since she and I went to Blackstar Station together. She didn't recognize me. I was wearing military pants, a camouflage jacket, and an old soldier's helmet. I suddenly felt the earliest sprouting of sweat poking through the seedlings of my pores.

from Giblet

Act i, scene i

   Giblet: *What mendacity is this that proclaimed itself thus upon my bereavement? It is a cold bluster of mind that turns to keep a man's soul from ascent.*

   Aide to Giblet: *Lo. Percival cometh my lord.*

Giblet (aside): Aye Percival come ye hither and taste my loinsword. Were ye a man like mine nuncle to whit perchance. But aye he has the eye of treachery about him. I shall make haste.

Percival: My lords.

Giblet (aside): Come ye. Come ye hither.

Aide to Giblet: The lord Percival my lord.

Giblet: What maketh a man such as ye daunt these furrowed shorebrows?

Percival: I distend alack my lord to thine blessed father and mine king.

Giblet (aside): Oh cold heart what yonder upon thee have I ever known but the curdling of noble blood? Mark this man to his stride upon me tether. To is or not to is. That be the question. Whether.

(unaside)

My blessed father and thine king is a treasure too rich for an asswit such as thyself. Let not thy cursed heart accustomgrown to thine ways caress me.

Percival: Giblet doth misstend his king's servant in thine own manner as to slander.

Enter Cassandra.

Cassandra: *My lords.*

Giblet, Percival (together): *Milady*

Cassandra: *Such fortune favor upon my stride. Mine must be the rosybuds of nudycheeks to in such presence be.*

Giblet (aside): *Oh Cassandra, thine heart is but a nibble upon mine shafted prawn. Enchantress that thou art so proud in thy mind's estimation.*

Percival: *Blessed Cassandra, give me thy nudycheeks as mine lips doth plot surrender.*

Cassandra: *And what of thee my lord Giblet? Have it not in thine pleasure to cast aside thy cruelty upon such matters?*

Enter Casablanca

Casablanca: *Lord Giblet! Lord Giblet! Untarry yourself hence my lord! The doctor has an acausation made.*

act i, scene ii

Giblet: *Oh father would that ought a man so conceived as thee to thine maker's eye, but savage nature upon thee has thrust its brazen stare. Oh cold hand.*

Doctor: He has the poisonlook about him my lord. Catch twinkle 'neath his shorebrows.

The Queen: And I now without kinghand to my comfort must my queenhand marry.

Giblet (aside): Oh what dark treachery waydles into this heart. Marry anon?

Percival: Oh cruel fate.

Giblet: It were but two days proclaimed of the king's death and ye speak anon of marriage mother?

The Queen: The kingdom needs a king, my child.

Giblet: I am none child mother that thou should address me so callous.

Percival: Yes, the kingdom needs a king my lord and dear queen so affronted by tragedy, I offer ye mine manhand for lessons in thy queenhand be.

Giblet: Surely an asswit indeed that offers such lamehand to my mommy be. You? King?!

The Queen: Hush now Giblet. Come with me Percival and I shall consider ye royal manhand fit for my queenhand be.

Giblet: *No man of foreign shorebrow shall be king while my father blows deathwind of a poisonous nature. Surely spy thee his murder mother?*

The Queen: *Murder?*

Giblet: *The doctor has plain bespoke of poison. Bespoke anon doctor.*

The Queen: *But the doctor bespoke none of murder. Did you doctor? Perchance it was poisoned foodstuff.*

The Doctor: *Aye my queen, poisoned foodstuff, perhaps figs. Perchance murder. Are those figs in your pocket Giblet?*

Cassandra (aside): *How now that thou should marry the queen with a marriage vow?*

Percival (aside): *All will be clear to thee my loaf. Love.*

Giblet: *But these figs are mine. Surely you are an asswit to think me capable of possessing figs of a poisonous nature.*

The Queen: *Casablanca, bring hasty arrest upon my troubled son.*

Giblet: *Such a marriage shall render sickness upon thy kingdom! Sickness! You have not seen the last of Giblet!*

act i, scene iii

At the jail

Giblet: *Oh cold night such as this as to bring chill upon a man's hangings. And but a window to enchant me thus to moonlight's calling.*

Brunhilde: *Giblet.*

Giblet: *How?*

Brunhilde: *Giblet.*

Giblet: *How now?*

Brunhilde: *It is your love outside yonder window speak.*

Giblet: *Brunhilde! Oh dark lament that thou should witness me thus.*

Brunhilde: *I broke window of mine father's keep to make haste herewith.*

Ghost of Giblet's father: *Giblet.*

Giblet: *How?*

Brunhilde: *I sayeth I broke window of mine father's keep to make haste herewith.*

Ghost of Giblet's father: *Giblet.*

Giblet: *How now?*

Brunhilde: *Boxeth they thine ears my love? I sayeth I broke wind—*

Giblet: *Not thee fair and loving Brunhilde. Alas the spirit voice of mine dead father and your dead king doth mount this tremulous air.*

Brunhilde: *Oh darling Giblet peer at my unhappy bosoms from aloft.*

Giblet: *I see them oh fair and loving Brunhilde.*

Ghost of Giblet's father: *I see them too oh fair and loving Brunhilde.*

Brunhilde: *Hark as east I turn to reveal full moon.*

Giblet: *I see Brunhilde. I see.*

Ghost of Giblet's father: *Unspeak thou thus and pray tell thee of mine demise.*

Giblet: *And what of the west oh fair and loving Brunhilde?*

Ghost of Giblet's father: *Unhinge thy eyes hence and recount what treachery from royal bosoms burst that I am dead? Pray tell thee Giblet.*

Giblet: *Mother poisoned thee with the dusky aide of Casablanca oh father. With figs.*

Brunhilde: *How?*

Ghost of Giblet's father: *How now what treachery thou bespoke?*

Giblet: *Were mine hands about her neck her life would be spittle upon sheepseth great father.*

Ghost of Giblet's father: *Oh no no no dear Giblet. No. Give thine king time here unwed. I beg thee. Do none such thing to thine treacherous mother. Your escape haste is front concern to thine crown command.*

Brunhilde: *Sing thee song of fair love my love. What am I without thee that I should dance on hot coals unshoed? Fever dear Giblet. Fever has upon mine skin overtaken. Are my hands not thine? Are my ears not thine? Is my heart not--*

Giblet: *Nude thyself oh fair and loving Brunhilde and make thee a rope of thine clothes that frometh this jail I should unencumber.*

Reading over other people's shoulders has taught me that there are consequences to reading anything written in a book out loud. I was on the train once going to Hanami Park when without thinking about it I started to read someone's book out loud. She didn't notice right away but at the second paragraph of the page she turned to me. I smiled because I was nervous. She smiled too. And then she started reading the book again, looking over her shoulder to me—welcoming me to give voice to the symbols printed upon the page. I read the last few paragraphs out loud to her. I moved behind her with my mouth very close to her ear. Her hair smelled of the past but with a freshness of the present (I smelled no future). But I read to her—loudly at first (to overcome the din) and then softly, almost to a whisper by the time the train had reached her stop. She closed the book and turned to look at me as she left the train. I think back to this moment and understand that this woman (whose name I didn't know and whose face

I couldn't remember) was and would always be my truest love.

My eyes turned to a sign near the cash register and without realizing it I had started to read the sign out loud. People looked up at me. Maria also looked up at me. She walked closer.

"You", she said. "That's crazy."

"It's okay everyone", the store manager said. "He's working."

"When do you finish working?" she asked me.

"Soon", I said—without trying to move my lips.

She pointed to her camera and said that she had some photographs to show me. Maybe her photographs will give me something. I suddenly felt as if I had nothing. Nothing filled me and I, in turn, filled nothing. Nothing in nature or books (my books or the books of others) or people. I had become detached which happened more frequently. I never stayed detached but each time I became detached I could never be sure that I would become attached again.

There are people I see who are being erased
from this world. When they are in this state I think
they are in a place called World A. It's a place in
which people are in the process of disappearing. In
somebody's world they may already be missing or
soon they will be gone and will never return. I live
in World A but I also live in a different world where
I can see those who are here and those who are in
the process of disappearing but not those who have
disappeared. I also want to name my world but I
can't think of a name to put to it. I think that
naming things makes it easier to connect with them.

What if I didn't know the woman's name was
Maria? It would have been more difficult to say:
Maria, I live across the street from the bus stop.
But I would have given her a name. If I didn't
know someone's name I assigned them a name in
my head. Perhaps just like my neighbor. The man
in the cigarette shop was Man 89. The gardener at
the house a few blocks away that I could see from
my window was Gardener 70. To look at another

human being in silence is easy. To look at one and have to speak is more difficult.

I said earlier that I had never felt the shame of being caught reading over someone's shoulder. But there was one time—I was on the left of a woman whose shoulder I was reading over and a man who caught me was on her right. The man looked at me several times. I could see half his face and one eye behind the woman's head. He whispered something into the woman's ear. She leaned closer to him to hear better and then she turned to me. I looked at her for a moment. I wanted her to think that I didn't know why she was looking at me but they made me feel guilty. She closed her book and held it by her side. So I have felt the shame of being caught. I couldn't say it earlier. It's difficult enough to feel the shame in one's self. I needed time to feel it and get rid of it before I could tell anyone about it. Reading out loud to the woman on the train made it possible for me to speak about my shame.

5: Bright Picture Lane

i

Maria still seems like a distant memory when I think of her. All that happened in the past I can never step into when I want to. I sometimes feel that if I focus on the memory and nothing else then maybe I could step into the memory whole and be there in the memory whole with the smallest details I didn't notice beforehand suddenly noticeable to me. The carpet fibres, the stack of unread books under the desk, the closet door slightly ajar (someone has forgotten to turn off the light in there). But I don't have this ability.

We were on the train together after a long day of taking photographs at the cemetery. I turned to Maria and told her that I was aware. I was aware of everything and everyone. She was sleeping. But I continued to speak to her as if she were awake.

"Your jawline", I whispered.

I heard her breathing. I looked out of the window that she leaned her head against and thought of myself sitting on the other side of it—on the outside of the train. From out there all would seem quiet in here. The world on the outside of the train would seem like the future. I would travel through different seasons quickly. Winter and snow. Spring and flowers. Summer and grass. Autumn and trees with heavy apples ready to pick. I would travel through platinum cities where buildings and sidewalks shimmered of glass and people always felt the slightest breeze cooling their eyebrows. A bumpy stretch of track would wake Maria up and she would see me through the window thinking that the image she saw was only a reflection of me sitting beside her but I was no longer there.

ii

Reading over someone's shoulder while I was travelling on the outside of the train (or bus) might distort the words on the pages because of the imperfections in the window glass. The reader and I would be reading two completely different texts and it could be argued by others (like me) that I wasn't reading over the person's shoulder at all because I was reading a different book—a book that didn't exist for the reader—in fact, a book that didn't exist for anyone else in the world and would never exist again after my brief encounter with it.

"I'm tired Maria", I said.

I didn't know how to explain my fixation without then saying good-bye to her (forever). I practiced in my head but my head was an illusion in which there was nowhere to practice explanations. No words of elaboration or dissemination or clarity could be formed. I practiced nothing related to speaking to her about my fixation so whenever I felt the urge to confess I could only put into action what I had practiced. I did nothing. I said nothing. And Maria would never understand or even know there was something to understand.

After the train ride I considered that we had taken three trips together and that it was time to ask her to come up to my apartment so I could show her my hummingbirds. They weren't mine I explained but they visited me like she would be visiting me.

This was the time of day they usually arrived to sup on the nectar I cooked up with a very specific formula of water and sugar—a concoction of my own formulation with which I attracted those hummingbirds that might be inclined to sup elsewhere. She accepted my invitation and upon entry to my apartment the slightest breeze cooled my hot eyebrows and I thought maybe this is the future I felt while I travelled on the outside of the train. I wondered if the breeze cooled her eyebrows also and if her eyebrows were, in fact, hot to begin with. I looked at them while she looked around. They looked hot. She put her bag and camera on the sofa.

Once when I was on an airplane going far away (I have been on an airplane many times) a man was sitting next to me reading a book called *The Sweet Way*. It was the only book that I read from cover to cover over someone's shoulder. I missed a page or two here and there because the way he held the book sometimes made it impossible for me to see the pages. It didn't seem like those missed pages were important but maybe they were. Maybe those few missed pages meant a completely different understanding of the story or ending for me than it did for him. He never slept, never ate the food they brought for him, never got up to go to the bathroom. He read the book from cover to cover with my eyes stealing every word he thought belonged only to him on that long flight. The book was about a husband and wife who grew plum trees on the farm they once used for peaches.

from Addinum

It has been said that the Croatian god created sugar plantations for the wing of man. The settee is a fine example. Defeated, I proclaimed victory for my undoing as I limped from her view. And then I whistled for my horse. It was, to put it humbly, the stuff of legends.

The astute among you may see this as the logical progression of a temperamental mix. Your shirt becomes covered in hair and oil (precisely f through l) and you think about your travels. Think about how every now and then you see an orange crane. But you don't see it for long. Not like when there were wigs and flasks of men going through trash cans for cigarellos and girls taking pictures and pictures being taken of girls (sitting on stairs). Pause. Relative relocation. Redefined boundaries. Fainting on the...fainting on the...but you (frank pensioneer) sat on that big pony and cut a fine swathe in the land. In that big fine caw of yours (my little piece of cheek (and same one round)).

We confessed that it was telling and we talked of the telling and she, unprized and luckless, had herself pinned naked to a/-tree. Perhaps she was glued.

But come my horsie and take me to Rotterdam. Life is good there. My whispers don't travel far. I could have saved her if I hadn't sullied her. But she had a swivel penchant for the macabre and said the clever made her sleepy. I said she was brain dead.

But sigh, her days stitch hum drum now. And hmm, we knew that. From here [that] done did that. Sit five [two] tree that. Fenster, sweet juicy jame, frairy, and our good friend Madame Jane Pimscot who ate bunny rabbit fritters the day her husband

died, I being an eyewitness to her having eaten
them, sodden and a bit early but she had the likes of
a craving in her [for them] for days upon days.

iii

I started going to the grocery store with only
one question in mind: what fruits would I offer to
Maria if she were to suddenly call to me from below
the open window and ask if she could come up to
my apartment? I walked the aisles slowly and paid
special attention to the more exotic fruits
(pomegranates, dragon fruits, figs). I didn't know
what fruits she liked. Nothing she ever said offered
any clues.

I thought that if I were a kid again I could ask
the girls who waited outside of the grocery store
and they would tell me what fruits to buy. One of
them would grab a basket and they would all run
into the grocery store with me (like they were
running from the beach into the ocean for the first
time at the start of summer) and move along the
fruit aisles picking out one of this fruit and one of

that fruit until I had a cornucopia of fruits of different colors and textures. But when you get older there aren't many people who want to help you with fruit selection. Maybe they think that all those years of going to the grocery store magically bestows upon you the necessary experience.

I bought apples, oranges, plums (nostalgia from reading *The Sweet Way*), cantaloupe, and raspberries. I left the apples and oranges on my small kitchen table so that when Maria walked in she would see the deep red and bright orange against the backdrop of my opened window. Perhaps at the opening of the door the hummingbirds would appear at the window to sup on the delicious nectar I concocted. But they didn't. Maria didn't want any fruits. We sat at the table and looked at the world outside.

When I am falling asleep I don't think about people or events. I think about plants growing—the evolution of their growth. The plants I most often think about are raspberries and grapes—their beginnings as little sticks and then after a few years strong enough to hold small fruits that look as if they might never grow but by the start or middle or end of summer have secretly grown to become what we know of them (the fruits plump and bright, the leaves and stems unruly and deserving of applause for the hard work they have done).

"Do you like dancing?" I asked.

I had some music albums I hadn't played in years. She showed me the photographs she had taken—from Hanami Park, from Blackstar Station, from my work (a photograph of me standing completely still with the soldier's helmet on). After we looked at all of the photographs she had taken she said she had to go. Even when she was walking through the door and looked back at me I thought the hummingbirds might appear like a surprise ending from a book. She would turn to say goodbye and then suddenly point to the window behind me. The poetry of that moment would have stayed with her forever. I watched her walk down the hallway. I heard the elevator door open and saw the lady who lived across the hall from me step out of the elevator and Maria step in. I closed my door and walked to the window. I watched Maria walk down the sidewalk until she disappeared from my view. I wish that watching her had some kind of meaning. I wish many things had meaning—like smoothing out the sheet on my bed with my hand or sitting down in a way that I thought showed my body's most beautiful form.

from Dear Diary Diary

Last night I wrote about my day (August 23, 2017) in my diary. My sturdy stylus pen ran out of ink. I thought that was very strange, considering I had only used it once. So instead I used a Sanford® Eagle® #2 pencil that I sharpened with the manual pencil sharpener that I keep on top of my unsigned copy of The Jit Motel. I plan to trace over last night's entry with a pen, preferably with black ink. And that's not all. I was also very disappointed because I noticed that I could see through the page of last night's entry to the naked woman I had drawn in the margin on the other side, even though I colored it over with a thick, black magic marker. The nipple really showed through. I think the paper in my diary is not up to snuff. I don't think I should be able to see through the paper to the other side of the page. But I flipped through the pages of my unsigned copy of The Jit Motel and I could see through that paper too. It's all very puzzling. I wasn't quite sure what I should do. It's like a mystery or something. I'll admit that it was a bumpy entry last night. The muffled noise coming from the closet distracted me. I tried to ignore it, but it wasn't easy. I almost got up and kicked the closet door in anger. But I can't wait until the future when someone reads what I wrote in my diary last night about what happened yesterday. I am giddy thinking about it. Shucks (I don't often write words like shucks in my diary), in spite of all that happened while I was writing in my diary, it turned out to be one of the most thrilling entries yet. Until tomorrow...

iv

After Maria left I realized that she never showed me any photographs that she took at the cemetery. I thought about talking to the woman who lived across the hall from me. I would finally tell her my real name. I wondered if she would be happy to finally know my real name. Would she be upset because I had waited so long before I told her the truth? How long would it take for her to become accustomed to calling me by my real name? Sometimes she might call me by the wrong name and then quickly correct herself. I felt that I had done her a slight for never having told her my real name and no matter how much I tried to make it up to her she would never be able to forgive me. She would smile and wave and speak to me as if nothing had happened but when she went home she would have her cup of coffee or tea and think about how I had waited so long before I told her. I knocked on her door. She invited me in.

"I have to tell you something", I said.

"What is it?" she asked.

"My real name—", I started.

"I know", she interrupted. She put her hand on my arm. "Is it okay if I call you what I call you?" she asked. "Does it make you feel bad?"

Did it make me feel bad that she called me by a name that wasn't mine? I thought back to all the times she had ever called out to me or I overheard her talking about me to someone else. The only time it made me feel bad was when I was trying to become the name. So no, it didn't make me feel bad when she called me by the name. In fact, the entire conversation I was having with her involved words I wanted to speak.

"No", I said. "It doesn't."

"Thank you", she said. "I saw that girl getting on to the elevator. Is she—?"

"No", I said. "I met her on the train."

She told me the reason she called me by another name and asked me to promise never to tell anyone.

6: Catch Power

i

There was a time (a series of moments connected over a few hours) when I thought I preferred reading books over people's shoulders instead of reading my own books in the normal way. I was on my way to Catch Power when the train came to a stop. There was an announcement that debris had to be cleared from the track and that it would take ten minutes. I had my own book and could have read without feeling any nausea since the train was at a standstill. Instead I stood near a man who was reading a book with—what I thought at the time—the most superb book paper I had ever seen. It looked like a landscape of the most subtle and nuanced topography. The edges of the pages were ever-so-slightly frayed to form a precipice from which the letters and symbols of the words written there jumped to the next page to form other words. And each turn of a page produced a sound—in that small space that surrounded the two of us—unlike any sound I had ever heard before (these are among the sounds of life—the sound of a page turning, the sound of blood escaping the body, the sound of smoke dissipating—that even the greatest musicians are unable to create). The man turned three pages in the time it took for the train to move again. In those three pages I read about war and the destruction of a great city and a woman who returned to the city while everyone else was leaving.

For a few minutes on the train I wondered if I would ever read a book again unless I was reading it over someone's shoulder. The thought left my head when I reached my stop. When I arrived home I immediately sat on the couch and opened the book I was reading (*Present, Etc.*). I read as smoothly and without distraction as I had always read. The thought of reading a book over someone's shoulder never occurred to me while I was reading my own book. I read like a man or a woman wakes up in the morning. The hummingbirds fluttered in and out of my open window to sup on the nectar I concocted.

I had satisfied myself as to the question of whether I preferred to read over someone's shoulder or read normally when it came to two different books. But I was never able to answer the question of whether I preferred to read a book over someone's shoulder or read it normally if it were the same book. I had a plan for how to answer the question but I thought there would be no way of putting the plan into action. It could happen quickly (*The Sweet Way*) or it could take multiple lifetimes and an alignment of random occurrences over those lifetimes as to make the question unanswerable. And still I was hopeful because I had read an entire book (*The Sweet Way*) over someone's shoulder that I then read afterwards. I only had to do the opposite—read a book normally and then read that same book over someone's shoulder—at some point in my life. It was a goal as worthy as any I could think of (except maybe for finding cures for deadly diseases, equality for the oppressed, eradicating poverty, or helping children). Recently I started to buy the books I have read over other people's shoulders and I have read the same parts of the books that I read over other people's shoulders but it has been difficult to ascertain which I prefer because I can only read a few pages.

from The History of Common Objects

As I walked I lamented my cowardice but recognized my lament as possibly a first step towards courage. I could tell you that I anticipated the vision of our house from the road and then something about who would have guessed that mother was sitting on the steps and that I could see her between the trees and that I was filled with insight and suddenly realized this or felt that, but I realized nothing and I felt nothing.

iii

I thought about raspberry bushes and grape vines when I fell asleep but more and more I thought about the woman I read to on the train.

82

Would she remember me and the circumstances of our encounter? Would she remember the feeling she had while I was reading the words from her book into her ear? I remembered her ear. I had looked directly at it and told myself to remember it. Maybe she wouldn't remember my face or any visual characteristics about me. Maybe she would remember my voice. That was possible. At the very least she would remember the time that someone read to her on the train. Maybe fifty years later. Maybe while she read to her grandchildren the memory would come to her. Or maybe she would try to push the memory away for some reason. She would try to attach other thoughts to it (the smell of the train, the trash can overflowing with trash in the station as she departed, the bacteria of a hundred people in a small space) to make it memorable in a bad way. She might try but the memory would stay with her and in time make itself good again so that when it ascended in her head above all other memories while she read to her grandchildren she might pause for a moment and have a good feeling before continuing. It would be cruel person indeed who would take such a thing from another person.

I hadn't seen Maria in months. Summer was over. Autumn had arrived. I remembered her disappearing into the elevator. I remembered looking out the window and seeing her walking away.

from Hell to Hellfire

Mr. Beauregard expressed his views on a napkin that he pushed across the table towards me. I imagined his skull and wondered when he would start calling me Fauntleroy. The poor man's memory was gone and he called everyone Fauntleroy after a while. I guess it was easier to keep track of Fauntleroys than a bevy of Johns or Jacks or Rudys. Some people said Fauntleroy was the name of a puppy he had when he was six years old but who the hell knows? Mr. Beauregard didn't speak much but he did have nice teeth.

I wondered why Maria never showed me the photographs of the cemetery we visited. I didn't visit graves (even of the people I knew) so it was a great undertaking for me. I wondered if there was someone there she wanted to visit but we didn't stop for a long time at any particular grave. We read the headstones as we moved along. Only our footsteps on the pavement disturbed those buried there. Whenever I felt like speaking I stayed quiet instead. I didn't want to be there and I also didn't want to leave.

I decided to go to the cemetery on my own and walk around to find something. I wanted to look for something. Anything. I wanted to be in search of something that I could keep in my GO Action Journal. A day to day search filled with failures and successes, of right turns and wrong turns, of exhilaration and exhaustion. I didn't find anything except the words I put together to describe a situation that (as far as I could tell) meant nothing.

7: The Armaments of Predictions

i

I was on the train to the Armaments of Predictions when I saw a woman who looked like Maria. But after so many months I couldn't be sure. I walked towards her but on my way I saw another woman reading a book. I stopped and stood behind her. I looked over her shoulder. I read with her until the next stop. My favorite books to read over other people's shoulders are books that I have never heard of, books that exist without fanfare, books that lie passively in wait. The woman was reading one of those books. When the train stopped I looked up to find Maria but she was gone. I alighted at the stop after the Armaments of Predictions.

When I went back to the cemetery I didn't know what I was looking for. I walked along the same path I thought Maria and I had walked. I looked at the headstones carefully to see if there was anything I could learn from them. Did any of them hold any clues about Maria? I couldn't find anything. I had even brought my GO Action Journal to write in but I only wrote a single paragraph.

I walked towards the Armaments of Predictions. If the woman was Maria then I missed her. I had missed her for all those months and now I would miss her again. I stopped in at several restaurants to look but I didn't find her. Maybe it wasn't her. But if it wasn't her then who was it? There were people out there who looked like Maria but they weren't Maria. In Budapest, for example, there may be ten or twenty people who look like Maria. One might be a small child, another an old grandfather. But people who look alike are not the same. Sometimes they are very different. That is the chaos of the world we live in.

ii

I decided to visit the part of the city I usually didn't visit. The part of the city that was ruined. The part of the city that Maria and I had visited together—Blackstar Station. I had never been there during the fall. I only went there when the weather was warm and there were leaves on the trees. But when the decay comes and the leaves start to fall from the trees, it's possible to see more and see further than through all the burgeoning lushness of new life. One can remember everything one had forgotten about. And then with the arrival of spring one can forget again. Like the spring and the fall, both remembering and forgetting are equally important. Sometimes I wanted to remember and sometimes I wanted to forget but I never practiced so I wasn't very good at remembering or forgetting. I was average.

I took the train back towards the Avenue of Children but got off at the Invention Gardens stop to go to the grocery store. I needed more fruits (just in case). I knew exactly where all the fruits were but I had been waiting for the grocery store to change its layout because I knew that grocery stores sometimes made changes. I always walked in (like a catbird) expecting to see that the apples had been moved (and maybe even the bananas) to another location within the store. Sometimes I thought that

89

deep in my subconscious I wished they were moved so I could feel slightly unsettled. I filled my basket with an assortment of fruits (strawberries, blueberries, raspberries, apples, pears, and grapes) stood in line to pay when I saw Maria and another woman talking together in another line. They were fourth in their line. I was third in mine. I spied the amount of groceries the people in front of me were buying. I spied the amount of groceries the people in front of Maria were buying. There were only three people in front of me but they seemed to have more groceries, although some of the groceries looked to be the same so the clerk would only have to put in the price for one of them and then the count instead of having to put the price for them separately. I wanted to finish paying for my groceries when Maria was just starting to pay for hers. I would walk by as she was picking up her bags and then I would offer to help her so that we might once again become entangled.

from The Sweet Way

What Mary learned the hard way had to do with ironing. Collars. Sleeves. The back of the shirt where the shoulder blades rubbed against. The creases. And although she disliked the steam from the iron it still gave her some small satisfaction because it made her think about her reflection at the bottom of the hot metal and how the steam seemed to surround her face with what she thought of as mystery.

Go see the world she would think to herself before pressing the iron against the wrinkled cuffs of another white shirt. She had pressed her face against many shirts and skirts and dresses and her face had been everywhere she had not. It had gone to parties, danced at balls, sat under trees at picnics, enjoyed plays, and even seen the Kings and Queens of small, neighboring countries. She had seen herself age at the bottom of that iron but each time she pressed the iron against another piece of cloth she felt she was smoothing away the years.

Oh god, she dropped the iron on her foot. It was a crisis for Mary because she had just started to iron a large tablecloth she was going to use to cover the large dining table in the main dining hall for the big dining party taking place at the house later that evening. She had impressed her face upon the cloth in a place where she was certain it could witness everything that might take place.

The horse boy and the silver cleaner carried her outside and across the estate to her room in the servant's house. All she could think about, besides the devastating, unrelenting pain was her iron and the tablecloth she had left on the ironing table. Who would finish ironing it? Would they still use it? It didn't make any sense for them to use another one she thought because they'd have to start the ironing process from the very beginning.

"Take me back", she said. "Take me back to the house. For God's sake. It's nothing."

They knew she couldn't stand on her own and made up some excuse about her foot needing to be looked at. But they were tired. It was tiring to clean silver and shoe horses and they thought when they heard the scream coming from the house it might provide a respite for them. They didn't think they'd have to carry Mary across the vast estate.

"Gotta get back to work", they said. "We'll send the doctor".

And they left her there with one shoe on and a foot that by any layman's eye looked busted.

Back at the main house the iron rested quietly on the ironing board and the tablecloth hung over the edge. The vast estate between Mary and her ironing seemed suspended in mid-afternoon. A silence overtook the gardens and the trees seemed to blow something ominous through her window. The grounds became covered with mist. It was as if the events of the rest of the day hinged on what Mary would do next. Mary. The vast, misty space. The iron and the tablecloth.

If only there were some device or machine she could speak into to tell the others at the main house to finish ironing the tablecloth and place it on the dining table in the dining hall. The thought helped brace her against the agonizing pain of her throbbing foot, but it also reminded her of the steam

93

and the iron and her face and how her face would miss everything that happened at dinner.

She was feeling light-headed and lay on her bed. She was sad but didn't cry because she knew there would be other dinners and other tablecloths to iron. Maybe it was fate she thought. Or destiny. Which was similar to fate but slightly different. She felt they were both appropriate. And besides she thought, her face was out there. It was out there seeing things. And then she wondered what she was thinking about. But she had to think about something she thought. She pulled herself up and sat on the bed to look out the window. Her eyes sparkled a light brown through the mist.

iii

I overheard Maria and the other woman talking as I was packing away my fruits.

"When I stop to think about the fun I'm having then I stop having fun", Maria said.

"I try not to think about it", the other woman said.

"When we were at the museum I'm not sure if I was having fun because I never stopped to think about the fun we were having", Maria said.

"I think we were having fun but maybe it wasn't fun enough to stop to think about it", the other woman said.

"It's probably better that the fun isn't so good that you have to stop to think about it. Maybe good fun is better than great fun", Maria said.

"We can try to not think about it", the other woman said.

"I'll try", Maria said.

"I'll try too", the other woman said.

I had a dream about Maria the night before I saw her at the grocery store. I dreamt we were walking through The 6 Cities together and she took out a book she had written and started reading it. Her name was written on the book but it wasn't *Maria* although I read it as *Maria*. I walked behind her, reading over her shoulder while I picked up other books and put them into the luxury bag I was carrying. I found the books in different places. On a streetlamp, against a store window, on someone's shoe, on the back of a bicycle, in the river, in World A. When I woke up I tried to remember the words I read over her shoulder. All I could remember was: *there's a girl in the corner who will disappear into the wall. Run outside.*

iv

I paid for my fruits. I saw Maria putting a peach into her bag. I walked slowly to time my arrival to her. As she moved away from the cashier I approached.

"Hi", I said. "It's been months since I've seen you."

She smiled at me.

"It has been a while", she said. "How are you? How was your summer?"

"It transitioned well into the fall", I said. "I like abrupt transitions but this year the transition was smooth which afterwards I felt was necessary considering my circumstances. How was your summer?"

"Good", she said. "It also transitioned well for me. This is my friend. Her name is Maria also."

"Nice to meet you", I said.

"You look familiar", the other woman said.

"I don't think I've met you before", I said.

"No, I've met you before", she said.

She took a book from her luxury bag, turned her back to me, and lifted her book up as if to read from it. I felt light-headed and caught myself from falling down right there on the floor of Invention Gardens Food Shop. I couldn't resist. I looked over her shoulder and read from her book. I forgot all that was around me. She turned her head to the side and looked at me.

"Out loud", she said.

I leaned in closer to her and whispered all the words I saw on the page in the sequence in which they were written there. Her hair smelled of the past but with a hint of the present. I looked at her ear. I thought I heard someone from behind me say that I had forgotten to take my bags of groceries.

GO Action Journal 1

What if the people buried here came back into a world where things that people laughed about had changed? What was funny for centuries or millennia was no longer funny. People instead laughed at the various sizes of circles or the results of how some numbers were added or multiplied. It would be a stranger world than if humans learned how to fly.

GO Action Journal 2

We've lost our way on planet earth but we can still dance together and sing together and laugh together and wander into the forest alone together. We can swim to the bottom of the river together and float up together. We can pretend that we've found our way together. We can pretend we live in a stable world together. We can pretend we understand ourselves. We can pretend we understand each other. We can have a small garden.

GO Action Journal 3

The flowers viewed at Hanami Park are many. They are not just limited to cherry trees or plum trees. There are flowering apple trees and strawberry plants that flower before the fruits appear. On the ground between the concrete paths are tulips. Sunflowers are scattered throughout the park. The flower viewing statue itself stands in a garden teeming with wild flowers. In my jacket button hole is a Transvaal daisy that I plucked on my way to Hanami Park. Rose bushes survive here throughout the year when among the beautiful decay of winter the roses stand out like drops of blood.

GO Action Journal 4

I write letters to my mother and father. I've said it many times: nobody writes letters anymore. When I write a letter I have to think about the person I am writing to. Writing letters to someone is better than talking to someone. There isn't much time to think about someone else when you're talking to them. A connection between two people is deeper when they write letters to each other. When I write a letter I can be contemplative and thoughtful. I don't have to rush. I can return after many days—after my earliest and most idle thoughts have ripened so that I am writing exactly what I feel or think in such a way that the person I am writing to enters my consciousness. I have never sent any of these letters. Having someone else in your consciousness is frightening.

GO Action Journal 5

There are people you meet in this world who will never become hard, whose skin will never toughen. They will go through life being broken again and again until they are left in pieces held together by the barest threads of what it is to be alive.

GO Action Journal 6

I also think about the world. Don't think that I never think about the world just because I think about reading over other people's shoulders (a lot). I receive my news about the world from reading newspapers and magazines over other people's shoulders. I can read the headlines on the front page of a newspaper and know everything that is happening and can converse with anyone about world events. I often do—transitioning seamlessly from one topic to another—as if I am nonchalantly concerned when in fact I am deeply concerned. I also think about ways that I can read over my own shoulder. I wonder if it is possible. I might be able to set up mirrors in such a way as to make it possible. In the world I am like all people.

GO Action Journal 7

I had asked Maria if she liked to dance. I don't know why. I don't think she heard me because she didn't answer. Almost every time I spoke I thought about what I had just spoken and realized I didn't want to speak it. I don't want to speak but I feel like others expect me to speak. And I speak words I don't want to speak. I don't always know what I want to speak and yet I speak in some kind of trial-and-error composition of words that barely have meaning to me beyond the sounds the letters make when put one after the other.

GO Action Journal 8

Thinking leads to questions and uncertainty—about our thoughts, about the construction of our thoughts. When I am a mannequin I think all the time. I stand completely still and do nothing but think while people walk around me. Sometimes I feel.

GO Action Journal 9

We may not be able to solve the mystery of our arrival but we may find, in the unraveling of the different layers of the mystery, something beautiful and possibly even useful. Perhaps the realization of our hopes is too young. When we are young we mistake our vitality for strength and sometimes cannot see how weak we are and how easily we can be taken advantage of by those miserable creatures who do nothing but seek their own advantage. But over time all of our realizations and achievements will age (they can only do so over time) and our ability to defend them will become strong.

GO Action Journal 10

I see the skull of every human person I talk to. I see the empty holes from which their eyes should outward jut. Sometimes I see pieces of hair still attached to the skull. I see the skulls with perfect teeth. I see their spines being formed one vertebra at a time as I am talking to them.

GO Action Journal 11

I ran outside. I walked through The 6 Cities by myself looking like I am always looking. I felt that I

was trying to protect someone or many people from
something in The 6 Cities, in World A, in the
Armaments of Predictions. But they were all dead.
In real life it's not possible to move into a wall and
disappear. In real life, though, sometimes they kill
everyone and leave no one behind. The city was
empty. Even I wasn't there.

GO Action Journal 12

My neighbor told me we can live in any world we
want to live in. The 6 Cities, World A, anywhere.
As long as the music in our head is loud enough.

The 6 Cities

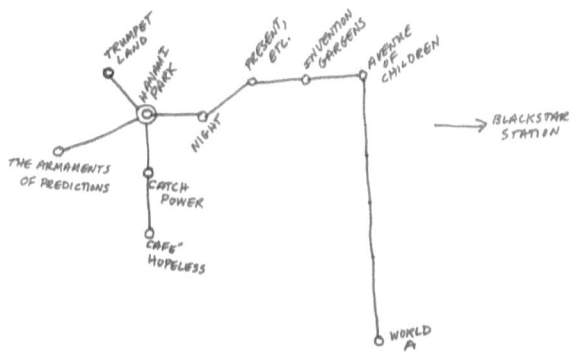

THE 6 CITIES

World A is farther away than it appears on the map. Blackstar Station cannot be reached by train. The train to Night from Present, Etc. travels on a bridge above the river.

www.ingramcontent.com/pod-product-compliance
Lightning Source LLC
Chambersburg PA
CBHW021928170626
46807CB00007B/3025